TENDER BUTTONS

Objects • Food • Rooms

Gertrude Stein

DOVER PUBLICATIONS, INC.
Mineola, New York

Copyright

Bibliographical Note

This Dover edition, first published in 1997, contains the unabridged text of the work first published by Claire Marie, New York, 1914. The Note was prepared specially for this edition.

Library of Congress Cataloging-in-Publication Data

Stein, Gertrude, 1874–1946.
Tender buttons : objects, food, rooms / Gertrude Stein.
p. cm.
ISBN 0-486-29897-3 (pbk.)
I. Title.
PS3537.T323T4 1997
811'.52—dc21

97-37232
CIP

Manufactured in the United States of America
Dover Publications, Inc., 31 East 2nd Street, Mineola, N.Y. 11501

NOTE

A determined literary experimenter, Gertrude Stein (1874–1946) encountered the resistance of mainstream culture to the new and the unconventional. Although *Tender Buttons* (1914) found a publisher in Claire Marie in New York, many of her works first made their way into print only through self-publication, or remained unpublished until after the author's death. But if Stein would always remain a writer more talked about than read, she did attain a considerable degree of popularity and recognition in her later years: the universities of Oxford and Cambridge repeatedly invited her to deliver lectures, and an American speaking-tour in 1934 brought her further acclaim.

Stein had been a student of the philosopher William James and shared his interest in automatic writing, an interest which perhaps shaped her own theories of composition. From the start she was determined to break away from literary tradition, although her first book, *Three Lives* (1904–5; published 1909), retained such narrative conventions as sentence structure and plot. Her next, *The Making of Americans* (1906–8; published 1925), while taking her into less-charted regions, still did not accomplish what she had in mind. Stein had been trying to create portraits of people, portraits rooted solely in the present moment, but as she progressed she

> got bothered, after all I listened and talked but that was not all I did in knowing at any present time when I was stating anything what anything was. I was also looking, and that could not be entirely left out.
>
> The trouble with including looking . . . was that in regard to human beings looking inevitably carried in its train realizing movements and expression and as such forced me into recognizing resemblances, and so forced remembering and in forcing remembering caused confusion of present with past and future time.[1]

1. This and the following quotes are taken from Stein's lecture "Portraits and Repetition," collected in *Gertrude Stein: Writings and Lectures,* Patricia Meyerowitz (ed.), Penguin Books, Inc., Baltimore, 1971.

She would need to reapproach this problem, and in writing her next pieces she came upon a solution.

Again she began to produce portraits, but now they were "portraits of rooms and food and everything because there I could avoid this difficulty of suggesting remembering more easily . . . than if I were to describe human beings." It was a shift in focus influenced in part by her many artist friends, Picasso and Bracque among them, who were attempting to accomplish in their mediums what Stein was striving for in hers:

> The painters naturally were looking . . . and they too had to be certain that looking was not confusing itself with remembering. Remembering with them takes the form of suggesting in their painting in place of having actually created the thing in itself that they are painting . . . I began to make portraits of things and enclosures that is rooms and places because I needed to completely face the difficulty of how to include what is seen with hearing and listening and at first if I were to include a complicated listening and talking it would be too difficult to do. That is why painters paint still lives.

Accompanying this change in subject was a change in vocabulary or, more precisely, a change in the way that she used words.

The portraits were published as *Tender Buttons,* and they revealed Stein to be attacking the denotations of words: while the individual elements of her sentences were familiar, their significance as a whole seemed to have been stripped away. She repeated words, recast them, rhymed them, and strung them together in unusual combinations. She emphasized their musical qualities, favoring sound over sense. Confronted with such unexpected associations and willful incoherence, the reader is forced to question the meanings of words, to become reacquainted with a language that Stein thought had become dulled by long use.

The experiment of *Tender Buttons* led Stein to her even more innovative work of the 1920s. While continuing to explore the possibilities of poetry (for such was her classification of *Tender Buttons*), she experimented further with prose writing, trying her hand at plays and operas as well. Although this work was largely ignored or ridiculed by the reading public, it served to inspire a new generation of writers (including Sherwood Anderson, Ernest Hemingway, and F. Scott Fitzgerald), prompting them to rethink the use of narrative, description, and even language itself.

From the 1930s onward Stein produced her most accessible and popular works, including the *Autobiography of Alice B. Toklas* (1933), *Everybody's Autobiography* (1937), and *Wars I Have Known* (1945). These autobiographical writings and the lecture tour of the same period have been seen by some critics as attempts at self-popularization: her return to the more lucid, conversational voice of *Three Lives* has similarly been regarded as an abandonment of her radical practices in favor of a style that would reach more readers. While there may be some truth in these observations, it was in fact these books (and the popular image of her as a mentor to young writers and as a patron of the arts) that kept Stein in the public memory until the 1970s, when the feminist movement began to champion her work. The subsequent reconsideration of her work has brought Stein recognition as a writer and innovator, and *Tender Buttons* is now appreciated as a landmark of twentieth-century literature.

CONTENTS

OBJECTS 1
FOOD. 19
ROOMS. 41

OBJECTS

A CARAFE, THAT IS A BLIND GLASS.

A kind in glass and a cousin, a spectacle and nothing strange a single hurt color and an arrangement in a system to pointing. All this and not ordinary, not unordered in not resembling. The difference is spreading.

GLAZED GLITTER.

Nickel, what is nickel, it is originally rid of a cover.

The change in that is that red weakens an hour. The change has come. There is no search. But there is, there is that hope and that interpretation and sometime, surely any is unwelcome, sometime there is breath and there will be a sinecure and charming very charming is that clean and cleansing. Certainly glittering is handsome and convincing.

There is no gratitude in mercy and in medicine. There can be breakages in Japanese. That is no programme. That is no color chosen. It was chosen yesterday, that showed spitting and perhaps washing and polishing. It certainly showed no obligation and perhaps if borrowing is not natural there is some use in giving.

A SUBSTANCE IN A CUSHION.

The change of color is likely and a difference a very little difference is prepared. Sugar is not a vegetable.

Callous is something that hardening leaves behind what will be soft if there is a genuine interest in there being present as many girls as men. Does this change. It shows that dirt is clean when there is a volume.

A cushion has that cover. Supposing you do not like to change, supposing it is very clean that there is no change in appearance, supposing that there is regularity and a costume is that any the worse than an oyster and an exchange. Come to season that is there any extreme use in feather and cotton. Is there not much more joy in a table and more chairs and very likely roundness and a place to put them.

A circle of fine card board and a chance to see a tassel.

What is the use of a violent kind of delightfulness if there is no pleasure in not getting tired of it. The question does not come before there is a quotation. In any kind of place there is a top to covering and it is a pleasure at any rate there is some venturing in refusing to believe nonsense. It shows what use there is in a whole piece if one uses it and it is extreme and very likely the little things could be dearer but in any case there is a bargain and if there is the best thing to do is to take it away and wear it and then be reckless be reckless and resolved on returning gratitude.

Light blue and the same red with purple makes a change. It shows that there is no mistake. Any pink shows that and very likely it is reasonable. Very likely there should not be a finer fancy present. Some increase means a calamity and this is the best preparation for three and more being together. A little calm is so ordinary and in any case there is sweetness and some of that.

A seal and matches and a swan and ivy and a suit.

A closet, a closet does not connect under the bed. The band if it is white and black, the band has a green string. A sight a whole sight and a little groan grinding makes a trimming such a sweet singing trimming and a red thing not a round thing but a white thing, a red thing and a white thing.

The disgrace is not in carelessness nor even in sewing it comes out out of the way.

What is the sash like. The sash is not like anything mustard it is not like a same thing that has stripes, it is not even more hurt than that, it has a little top.

A BOX.

Out of kindness comes redness and out of rudeness comes rapid same question, out of an eye comes research, out of selection comes painful cattle. So then the order is that a white way of being round is something suggesting a pin and is it disappointing, it is not, it is so rudimentary to be analysed and see a fine substance strangely, it is so earnest to have a green point not to red but to point again.

A PIECE OF COFFEE.

More of double.

A place in no new table.

A single image is not splendor. Dirty is yellow. A sign of more in not mentioned. A piece of coffee is not a detainer. The resemblance to yellow is dirtier and distincter. The clean mixture is whiter and not coal color, never more coal color than altogether.

The sight of a reason, the same sight slighter, the sight of a simpler negative answer, the same sore sounder, the intention to wishing, the same splendor, the same furniture.

The time to show a message is when too late and later there is no hanging in a blight.

A not torn rose-wood color. If it is not dangerous then a pleasure and more than any other if it is cheap is not cheaper. The amusing side is that the sooner there are no fewer the more certain is the necessity dwindled. Supposing that the case contained rose-wood and a color. Supposing that there was no reason for a distress and more likely for a number, supposing that there was no astonishment, is it not necessary to mingle astonishment.

The settling of stationing cleaning is one way not to shatter scatter and scattering. The one way to use custom is to use soap and silk for cleaning. The one way to see cotton is to have a design concentrating the illusion and the illustration. The perfect way is to accustom the thing to have a lining and the shape of a ribbon and to be solid, quite solid in standing and to use heaviness in morning. It is light enough in that. It has that shape nicely. Very nicely may not be exaggerating. Very strongly may be sincerely fainting. May be strangely flattering. May not be strange in everything. May not be strange to.

DIRT AND NOT COPPER.

Dirt and not copper makes a color darker. It makes the shape so heavy and makes no melody harder.

It makes mercy and relaxation and even a strength to spread a table fuller. There are more places not empty. They see cover.

NOTHING ELEGANT.

A charm a single charm is doubtful. If the red is rose and there is a gate surrounding it, if inside is let in and there places change then certainly something is upright. It is earnest.

MILDRED'S UMBRELLA.

A cause and no curve, a cause and loud enough, a cause and extra a loud clash and an extra wagon, a sign of extra, a sac a small sac and an established color and cunning, a slender grey and no ribbon, this means a loss a great loss a restitution.

A METHOD OF A CLOAK.

A single climb to a line, a straight exchange to a cane, a desperate adventure and courage and a clock, all this which is a system, which has feeling, which has resignation and success, all makes an attractive black silver.

A RED STAMP.

If lilies are lily white if they exhaust noise and distance and even dust, if they dusty will dirt a surface that has no extreme grace, if they do this and it is not necessary it is not at all necessary if they do this they need a catalogue.

A BOX.

A large box is handily made of what is necessary to replace any substance. Suppose an example is necessary, the plainer it is made the more reason there is for some outward recognition that there is a result.

A box is made sometimes and them to see to see to it neatly and to have the holes stopped up makes it necessary to use paper.

A custom which is necessary when a box is used and taken is that a large part of the time there are three which have different connections. The one is on the table. The two are on the table. The three are on the table. The one, one is the same length as is shown by the cover being longer. The other is different there is more cover that shows it. The other is different and that makes the corners have the same shade the eight are in singular arrangement to make four necessary.

Lax, to have corners, to be lighter than some weight, to indicate a wedding journey, to last brown and not curious, to be wealthy, cigarettes are established by length and by doubling.

Left open, to be left pounded, to be left closed, to be circulating in summer and winter, and sick color that is grey that is not dusty and red shows, to be sure cigarettes do measure an empty length sooner than a choice in color.

Winged, to be winged means that white is yellow and pieces pieces that are brown are dust color if dust is washed off, then it is choice that is to say it is fitting cigarettes sooner than paper.

An increase why is an increase idle, why is silver cloister, why is the spark brighter, if it is brighter is there any result, hardly more than ever.

A PLATE.

An occasion for a plate, an occasional resource is in buying and how soon does washing enable a selection of the same thing neater. If the party is small a clever song is in order.

Plates and a dinner set of colored china. Pack together a string and enough with it to protect the centre, cause a considerable haste and gather more as it is cooling, collect more trembling and not any even trembling, cause a whole thing to be a church.

A sad size a size that is not sad is blue as every bit of blue is precocious. A kind of green a game in green and nothing flat nothing quite flat and more round, nothing a particular color strangely, nothing breaking the losing of no little piece.

A splendid address a really splendid address is not shown by giving a flower freely, it is not shown by a mark or by wetting.

Cut cut in white, cut in white so lately. Cut more than any other and show it. Show it in the stem and in starting and in evening coming complication.

A lamp is not the only sign of glass. The lamp and the cake are not the only sign of stone. The lamp and the cake and the cover are not the only necessity altogether.

A plan a hearty plan, a compressed disease and no coffee, not even a card or a change to incline each way, a plan that has that excess and that break is the one that shows filling.

A SELTZER BOTTLE.

Any neglect of many particles to a cracking, any neglect of this makes around it what is lead in color and certainly discolor in silver. The use of this is manifold. Supposing a certain time selected is assured, suppose it is even necessary, suppose no other extract is permitted and no more handling is needed, suppose the rest of the message is mixed with a very long slender needle and even if it could be any black border, supposing all this altogether made a dress and suppose it was actual, suppose the mean way to state it was occasional, if you suppose this in August and even more melodiously, if you suppose this even in the necessary incident of there certainly being no middle in summer and winter, suppose this and an elegant settlement a very elegant settlement is more than of consequence, it is not final and sufficient and substituted. This which was so kindly a present was constant.

A LONG DRESS.

What is the current that makes machinery, that makes it crackle, what is the current that presents a long line and a necessary waist. What is this current.

What is the wind, what is it.

Where is the serene length, it is there and a dark place is not a dark place, only a white and red are black, only a yellow and green are blue, a pink is scarlet, a bow is every color. A line distinguishes it. A line just distinguishes it.

A RED HAT.

A dark grey, a very dark grey, a quite dark grey is monstrous ordinarily, it is so monstrous because there is no red in it. If red is in everything it is not necessary. Is that not an argument for any use of it and even so is there any place that is better, is there any place that has so much stretched out.

A BLUE COAT.

A blue coat is guided guided away, guided and guided away, that is the particular color that is used for that length and not any width not even more than a shadow.

A PIANO.

If the speed is open, if the color is careless, if the selection of a strong scent is not awkward, if the button holder is held by all the waving color and there is no color, not any color. If there is no dirt in a pin and there can be none scarcely, if there is not then the place is the same as up standing.

This is no dark custom and it even is not acted in any such a way that a restraint is not spread. That is spread, it shuts and it lifts and awkwardly not awkwardly the centre is in standing.

A CHAIR.

A widow in a wise veil and more garments shows that shadows are even. It addresses no more, it shadows the stage and learning. A regular arrangement, the severest and the most preserved is that which has the arrangement not more than always authorised.

A suitable establishment, well housed, practical, patient and staring, a suitable bedding, very suitable and not more particularly than complaining, anything suitable is so necessary.

A fact is that when the direction is just like that, no more, longer, sudden and at the same time not any sofa, the main action is that without a blaming there is no custody.

Practice measurement, practice the sign that means that really means a necessary betrayal, in showing that there is wearing.

Hope, what is a spectacle, a spectacle is the resemblance between the circular side place and nothing else, nothing else.

To choose it is ended, it is actual and more than that it has it certainly has the same treat, and a seat all that is practiced and more easily much more easily ordinarily.

Pick a barn, a whole barn, and bend more slender accents than have ever been necessary, shine in the darkness necessarily.

Actually not aching, actually not aching, a stubborn bloom is so artificial and even more than that, it is a spectacle, it is a binding accident, it is animosity and accentuation.

If the chance to dirty diminishing is necessary, if it is why is there no complexion, why is there no rubbing, why is there no special protection.

A FRIGHTFUL RELEASE.

A bag which was left and not only taken but turned away was not found. The place was shown to be very like the last time. A piece was not exchanged, not a bit of it, a piece was left over. The rest was mismanaged.

A PURSE.

A purse was not green, it was not straw color, it was hardly seen and it had a use a long use and the chain, the chain was never missing, it was not misplaced, it showed that it was open, that is all that it showed.

A MOUNTED UMBRELLA.

What was the use of not leaving it there where it would hang what was the use if there was no chance of ever seeing it come there and show that it was handsome and right in the way it showed it. The lesson is to learn that it does show it, that it shows it and that nothing, that there is nothing, that there is no more to do about it and just so much more is there plenty of reason for making an exchange.

A CLOTH.

Enough cloth is plenty and more, more is almost enough for that and besides if there is no more spreading is there plenty of room for it. Any occasion shows the best way.

MORE.

An elegant use of foliage and grace and a little piece of white cloth and oil.

Wondering so winningly in several kinds of oceans is the reason that makes red so regular and enthusiastic. The reason that there is more snips are the same shining very colored rid of no round color.

A NEW CUP AND SAUCER.

Enthusiastically hurting a clouded yellow bud and saucer, enthusiastically so is the bite in the ribbon.

OBJECTS.

Within, within the cut and slender joint alone, with sudden equals and no more than three, two in the centre make two one side.

If the elbow is long and it is filled so then the best example is all together.

The kind of show is made by squeezing.

EYE GLASSES.

A color in shaving, a saloon is well placed in the centre of an alley.

CUTLET.

A blind agitation is manly and uttermost.

CARELESS WATER.

No cup is broken in more places and mended, that is to say a plate is broken and mending does do that it shows that culture is Japanese. It shows the whole element of angels and orders. It does more to choosing and it does more to that ministering counting. It does, it does change in more water.

Supposing a single piece is a hair supposing more of them are orderly, does that show that strength, does that show that joint, does that show that balloon famously. Does it.

A PAPER.

A courteous occasion makes a paper show no such occasion and this makes readiness and eyesight and likeness and a stool.

A DRAWING.

The meaning of this is entirely and best to say the mark, best to say it best to show sudden places, best to make bitter, best to make the length tall and nothing broader, anything between the half.

WATER RAINING.

Water astonishing and difficult altogether makes a meadow and a stroke.

COLD CLIMATE.

A season in yellow sold extra strings makes lying places.

MALACHITE.

The sudden spoon is the same in no size. The sudden spoon is the wound in the decision.

AN UMBRELLA.

Coloring high means that the strange reason is in front not more in front behind. Not more in front in peace of the dot.

A PETTICOAT.

A light white, a disgrace, an ink spot, a rosy charm.

A WAIST.

A star glide, a single frantic sullenness, a single financial grass greediness.

Object that is in wood. Hold the pine, hold the dark, hold in the rush, make the bottom.

A piece of crystal. A change, in a change that is remarkable there is no reason to say that there was a time.

A woolen object gilded. A country climb is the best disgrace, a couple of practices any of them in order is so left.

A TIME TO EAT.

A pleasant simple habitual and tyrannical and authorised and educated and resumed and articulate separation. This is not tardy.

A LITTLE BIT OF A TUMBLER.

A shining indication of yellow consists in there having been more of the same color than could have been expected when all four were bought. This was the hope which made the six and seven have no use for any more places and this necessarily spread into nothing. Spread into nothing.

A FIRE.

What was the use of a whole time to send and not send if there was to be the kind of thing that made that come in. A letter was nicely sent.

A HANDKERCHIEF.

A winning of all the blessings, a sample not a sample because there is no worry.

RED ROSES.

A cool red rose and a pink cut pink, a collapse and a sold hole, a little less hot.

IN BETWEEN.

In between a place and candy is a narrow foot-path that shows more mounting than anything, so much really that a calling meaning a bolster measured a whole thing with that. A virgin a whole virgin is judged made and so between curves and outlines and real seasons and more out glasses and a perfectly unprecedented arrangement between old ladies and mild colds there is no satin wood shining.

COLORED HATS.

Colored hats are necessary to show that curls are worn by an addition of blank spaces, this makes the difference between single lines and broad stomachs, the least thing is lightening, the least thing means a little flower and a big delay a big delay that makes more nurses than little women really little women. So clean is a light that nearly all of it shows pearls and little ways. A large hat is tall and me and all custard whole.

A FEATHER.

A feather is trimmed, it is trimmed by the light and the bug and the post, it is trimmed by little leaning and by all sorts of mounted reserves and loud volumes. It is surely cohesive.

A BROWN.

A brown which is not liquid not more so is relaxed and yet there is a change, a news is pressing.

A LITTLE CALLED PAULINE.

A little called anything shows shudders.

Come and say what prints all day. A whole few watermelon. There is no pope.

No cut in pennies and little dressing and choose wide soles and little spats really little spices.

A little lace makes boils. This is not true.

Gracious of gracious and a stamp a blue green white bow a blue green lean, lean on the top.

If it is absurd then it is leadish and nearly set in where there is a tight head.

A peaceful life to arise her, noon and moon and moon. A letter a cold sleeve a blanket a shaving house and nearly the best and regular window.

Nearer in fairy sea, nearer and farther, show white has lime in sight, show a stitch of ten. Count, count more so that thicker and thicker is leaning.

I hope she has her cow. Bidding a wedding, widening received treading, little leading mention nothing.

Cough out cough out in the leather and really feather it is not for.

Please could, please could, jam it not plus more sit in when.

A SOUND.

Elephant beaten with candy and little pops and chews all bolts and reckless reckless rats, this is this.

A TABLE.

A table means does it not my dear it means a whole steadiness. Is it likely that a change.

A table means more than a glass even a looking glass is tall. A table means necessary places and a revision a revision of a little thing it means it does mean that there has been a stand, a stand where it did shake.

SHOES.

To be a wall with a damper a stream of pounding way and nearly enough choice makes a steady midnight. It is pus.

A shallow hole rose on red, a shallow hole in and in this makes ale less. It shows shine.

A DOG.

A little monkey goes like a donkey that means to say that means to say that more sighs last goes. Leave with it. A little monkey goes like a donkey.

A WHITE HUNTER.

A white hunter is nearly crazy.

A LEAVE.

In the middle of a tiny spot and nearly bare there is a nice thing to say that wrist is leading. Wrist is leading.

SUPPOSE AN EYES.

Suppose it is within a gate which open is open at the hour of closing summer that is to say it is so.

All the seats are needing blackening. A white dress is in sign. A soldier a real soldier has a worn lace a worn lace of different sizes that is to say if he can read, if he can read he is a size to show shutting up twenty-four.

Go red go red, laugh white.

Suppose a collapse in rubbed purr, in rubbed purr get.

Little sales ladies little sales ladies little saddles of mutton.

Little sales of leather and such beautiful beautiful, beautiful beautiful.

A SHAWL.

A shawl is a hat and hurt and a red balloon and an under coat and a sizer a sizer of talks.

A shawl is a wedding, a piece of wax a little build. A shawl.

Pick a ticket, pick it in strange steps and with hollows. There is hollow hollow belt, a belt is a shawl.

A plate that has a little bobble, all of them, any so.

Please a round it is ticket.

It was a mistake to state that a laugh and a lip and a laid climb and a depot and a cultivator and little choosing is a point it.

BOOK.

Book was there, it was there. Book was there. Stop it, stop it, it was a cleaner, a wet cleaner and it was not where it was wet, it was not high, it was directly placed back, not back again, back it was returned, it was needless, it put a bank, a bank when, a bank care.

Suppose a man a realistic expression of resolute reliability suggests pleasing itself white all white and no head does that mean soap. It does not so. It means kind wavers and little chance to beside beside rest. A plain.

Suppose ear rings, that is one way to breed, breed that. Oh chance to say, oh nice old pole. Next best and nearest a pillar. Chest not valuable, be papered.

Cover up cover up the two with a little piece of string and hope rose and green, green.

Please a plate, put a match to the seam and really then really then, really then it is a remark that joins many many lead games. It is a sister and sister and a flower and a flower and a dog and a colored sky a sky colored grey and nearly that nearly that let.

PEELED PENCIL, CHOKE.

Rub her coke.

IT WAS BLACK, BLACK TOOK.

Black ink best wheel bale brown.

Excellent not a hull house, not a pea soup, no bill no care, no precise no past pearl pearl goat.

THIS IS THE DRESS, AIDER.

Aider, why aider why whow, whow stop touch, aider whow, aider stop the muncher, muncher munchers.

A jack in kill her, a jack in, makes a meadowed king, makes a to let.

FOOD

ROASTBEEF; MUTTON; BREAKFAST; SUGAR; CRANBERRIES; MILK; EGGS; APPLE; TAILS; LUNCH; CUPS; RHUBARB; SINGLE; FISH; CAKE; CUSTARD; POTATOES; ASPARAGUS; BUTTER; END OF SUMMER; SAUSAGES; CELERY; VEAL; VEGETABLE; COOKING; CHICKEN; PASTRY; CREAM; CUCUMBER; DINNER; DINING; EATING; SALAD; SAUCE; SALMON; ORANGE; COCOA; AND CLEAR SOUP AND ORANGES AND OATMEAL; SALAD DRESSING AND AN ARTICHOKE; A CENTRE IN A TABLE.

ROASTBEEF.

In the inside there is sleeping, in the outside there is reddening, in the morning there is meaning, in the evening there is feeling. In the evening there is feeling. In feeling anything is resting, in feeling anything is mounting, in feeling there is resignation, in feeling there is recognition, in feeling there is recurrence and entirely mistaken there is pinching. All the standards have steamers and all the curtains have bed linen and all the yellow has discrimination and all the circle has circling. This makes sand.

Very well. Certainly the length is thinner and the rest, the round rest has a longer summer. To shine, why not shine, to shine, to station, to enlarge, to hurry the measure all this means nothing if there is singing, if there is singing then there is the resumption.

The change the dirt, not to change dirt means that there is no beefsteak and not to have that is no obstruction, it is so easy to exchange meaning, it is so easy to see the difference. The difference is that a plain resource is not entangled with thickness and it does not mean that thickness shows such cutting, it does mean that a meadow is useful and a cow absurd. It does not mean that there are tears, it does not mean that exudation is cumbersome, it means no more than a memory, a choice and a reëstablishment, it means more than any escape from a surrounding extra. All the time that there is use there is use and any time there is a surface there is a surface, and every time there is an exception there is an exception and every time there is a division there is a dividing. Any time there is a surface there is a surface and every time there is a suggestion there is a suggestion and every time there is silence there is silence and every time that is languid there is that there then and not oftener, not always, not particular, tender and changing and external and central and surrounded and singular and simple and the same and the surface and the circle and the shine and the succor and the white and the same and the better and the red and the same and the centre and the yellow and the tender and the better, and altogether.

Considering the circumstances there is no occasion for a reduction, considering that there is no pealing there is no occasion for an obligation, considering that there is no outrage there is no necessity for any reparation, considering that there is no particle sodden there is no occasion for deliberation. Considering everything and which way the turn is tending, considering everything why is there no restraint, considering everything what makes the place settle and the plate distinguish some specialties. The whole thing is not understood and this is not strange considering that there is no education, this is not strange because having that certainly does show the difference in cutting, it shows that when there is turning there is no distress.

In kind, in a control, in a period, in the alteration of pigeons, in kind cuts and thick and thin spaces, in kind ham and different colors, the length of leaning a strong thing outside not to make a sound but to suggest a crust, the principal taste is when there is a whole chance to be reasonable, this does not mean that there is overtaking, this means nothing precious, this means clearly that the chance to exercise is a social success. So then the sound is not obtrusive. Suppose it is obtrusive suppose it is. What is certainly the desertion is not a reduced description, a description is not a birthday.

Lovely snipe and tender turn, excellent vapor and slender butter, all the splinter and the trunk, all the poisonous darkening drunk, all the joy in weak success, all the joyful tenderness, all the section and the tea, all the stouter symmetry.

Around the size that is small, inside the stern that is the middle, besides the remains that are praying, inside the between that is turning, all the region is measuring and melting is exaggerating.

Rectangular ribbon does not mean that there is no eruption it means that if there is no place to hold there is no place to spread. Kindness is not earnest, it is not assiduous it is not revered.

Room to comb chickens and feathers and ripe purple, room to curve single plates and large sets and second silver, room to send everything away, room to save heat and distemper, room to search a light that is simpler, all room has no shadow.

There is no use there is no use at all in smell, in taste, in teeth, in toast, in anything, there is no use at all and the respect is mutual.

Why should that which is uneven, that which is resumed, that which is tolerable why should all this resemble a smell, a thing is there, it whistles, it is not narrower, why is there no obligation to stay away and yet courage, courage is everywhere and the best remains to stay.

If there could be that which is contained in that which is felt there would be a chair where there are chairs and there would be no more denial about a clatter. A clatter is not a smell. All this is good.

The Saturday evening which is Sunday is every week day. What choice is there when there is a difference. A regulation is not active. Thirstiness is not equal division.

Anyway, to be older and ageder is not a surfeit nor a suction, it is not dated and careful, it is not dirty. Any little thing is clean, rubbing is black. Why should ancient lambs be goats and young colts and never beef, why should they, they should because there is so much difference in age.

A sound, a whole sound is not separation, a whole sound is in an order.

Suppose there is a pigeon, suppose there is.

Looseness, why is there a shadow in a kitchen, there is a shadow in a kitchen because every little thing is bigger.

The time when there are four choices and there are four choices in a difference, the time when there are four choices there is a kind and there is a kind. There is a kind. There is a kind. Supposing there is a bone, there is a bone. Supposing there are bones. There are bones. When there are bones there is no supposing there are bones. There are bones and there is that consuming. The kindly way to feel separating is to have a space between. This shows a likeness.

Hope in gates, hope in spoons, hope in doors, hope in tables, no hope in daintiness and determination. Hope in dates.

Tin is not a can and a stove is hardly. Tin is not necessary and neither is a stretcher. Tin is never narrow and thick.

Color is in coal. Coal is outlasting roasting and a spoonful, a whole spoon that is full is not spilling. Coal any coal is copper.

Claiming nothing, not claiming anything, not a claim in everything, collecting claiming, all this makes a harmony, it even makes a succession.

Sincerely gracious one morning, sincerely graciously trembling, sincere in gracious eloping, all this makes a furnace and a blanket. All this shows quantity.

Like an eye, not so much more, not any searching, no compliments.

Please be the beef, please beef, pleasure is not wailing. Please beef, please be carved clear, please be a case of consideration.

Search a neglect. A sale, any greatness is a stall and there is no memory, there is no clear collection.

A satin sight, what is a trick, no trick is mountainous and the color, all the rush is in the blood.

Bargaining for a little, bargain for a touch, a liberty, an estrangement, a characteristic turkey.

Please spice, please no name, place a whole weight, sink into a standard rising, raise a circle, choose a right around, make the resonance accounted and gather green any collar.

To bury a slender chicken, to raise an old feather, to surround a garland and to bake a pole splinter, to suggest a repose and to settle simply, to surrender one another, to succeed saving simpler, to satisfy a singularity and not to be blinder, to sugar nothing darker and to read redder, to have the color better, to sort out dinner, to remain together, to surprise no sinner, to curve nothing sweeter, to continue thinner, to increase in resting recreation to design string not dimmer.

Cloudiness what is cloudiness, is it a lining, is it a roll, is it melting.

The sooner there is jerking, the sooner freshness is tender, the sooner the round it is not round the sooner it is withdrawn in cutting, the sooner the measure means service, the sooner there is chinking, the sooner there is sadder than salad, the sooner there is none do her, the sooner there is no choice, the sooner there is a gloom freer, the same sooner and more sooner, this is no error in hurry and in pressure and in opposition to consideration.

A recital, what is a recital, it is an organ and use does not strengthen valor, it soothes medicine.

A transfer, a large transfer, a little transfer, some transfer, clouds and tracks do transfer, a transfer is not neglected.

Pride, when is there perfect pretence, there is no more than yesterday and ordinary.

A sentence of a vagueness that is violence is authority and a mission and stumbling and also certainly also a prison. Calmness, calm is beside the plate and in way in. There is no turn in terror. There is no volume in sound.

There is coagulation in cold and there is none in prudence.

Something is preserved and the evening is long and the colder spring has sudden shadows in a sun. All the stain is tender and lilacs really lilacs are disturbed. Why is the perfect reëstablishment practiced and prized, why is it composed. The result the pure result is juice and size and baking and exhibition and nonchalance and sacrifice and volume and a section in division and the surrounding recognition and horticulture and no murmur. This is a result. There is no superposition and circumstance, there is hardness and a reason and the rest and remainder. There is no delight and no mathematics.

MUTTON.

A letter which can wither, a learning which can suffer and an outrage which is simultaneous is principal.

Student, students are merciful and recognised they chew something.

Hate rests that is solid and sparse and all in a shape and largely very largely. Interleaved and successive and a sample of smell all this makes a certainty a shade.

Light curls very light curls have no more curliness than soup. This is not a subject.

Change a single stream of denting and change it hurriedly, what does it express, it expresses nausea. Like a very strange likeness and pink, like that and not more like that than the same resemblance and not more like that than no middle space in cutting.

An eye glass, what is an eye glass, it is water. A splendid specimen, what is it when it is little and tender so that there are parts. A centre can place and four are no more and two and two are not middle.

Melting and not minding, safety and powder, a particular recollection and a sincere solitude all this makes a shunning so thorough and so unrepeated and surely if there is anything left it is a bone. It is not solitary.

Any space is not quiet it is so likely to be shiny. Darkness very dark darkness is sectional. There is a way to see in onion and surely very surely rhubarb and a tomato, surely very surely there is that seeding. A little thing in is a little thing.

Mud and water were not present and not any more of either. Silk and stockings were not present and not any more of either. A receptacle and a symbol and no monster were present and no more. This made a piece show and was it a kindness, it can be asked was it a kindness to have it warmer, was it a kindness and does gliding mean more. Does it.

Does it dirty a ceiling. It does not. Is it dainty, it is if prices are sweet. Is it lamentable, it is not if there is no undertaker. Is it curious, it is not when there is youth. All this makes a line, it even makes makes no more. All this makes cherries. The reason that there is a suggestion in vanity is due to this that there is a burst of mixed music.

A temptation any temptation is an exclamation if there are misdeeds and little bones. It is not astonishing that bones mingle as they vary not at all and in any case why is a bone outstanding, it is so because the circumstance that does not make a cake and character is so easily churned and cherished.

Mouse and mountain and a quiver, a quaint statue and pain in an exterior and silence more silence louder shows salmon a mischief intender. A cake, a real salve made of mutton and liquor, a specially retained rinsing and an established cork and blazing, this which resignation influences and restrains, restrains more altogether. A sign is the specimen spoken.

A meal in mutton, mutton, why is lamb cheaper, it is cheaper because so little is more. Lecture, lecture and repeat instruction.

BREAKFAST.

A change, a final change includes potatoes. This is no authority for the abuse of cheese. What language can instruct any fellow.

A shining breakfast, a breakfast shining, no dispute, no practice, nothing, nothing at all.

A sudden slice changes the whole plate, it does so suddenly.

An imitation, more imitation, imitation succeed imitations.

Anything that is decent, anything that is present, a calm and a cook and more singularly still a shelter, all these show the need of clamor. What is the custom, the custom is in the centre.

What is a loving tongue and pepper and more fish than there is when tears many tears are necessary. The tongue and the salmon, there is not salmon when brown is a color, there is salmon when there is no meaning to an early morning being pleasanter. There is no salmon, there are no tea-cups, there are the same kind of mushes as are used as stomachers by the eating hopes that makes eggs delicious. Drink is likely to stir a certain respect for an egg cup and more water melon than was ever eaten yesterday. Beer is neglected and cocoanut is famous. Coffee all coffee and a sample of soup all soup these are the choice of a baker. A white cup means a wedding. A wet cup means a vacation. A strong cup means an especial regulation. A single cup means a capital arrangement between the drawer and the place that is open.

Price a price is not in language, it is not in custom, it is not in praise.

A colored loss, why is there no leisure. If the persecution is so outrageous that nothing is solemn is there any occasion for persuasion.

A grey turn to a top and bottom, a silent pocketful of much heating, all the pliable succession of surrendering makes an ingenious joy.

A breeze in a jar and even then silence, a special anticipation in a rack, a gurgle a whole gurgle and more cheese than almost anything, is this an astonishment, does this incline more than the original division between a tray and a talking arrangement and even then a calling into another room gently with some chicken in any way.

A bent way that is a way to declare that the best is all together, a bent way shows no result, it shows a slight restraint, it shows a necessity for retraction.

Suspect a single buttered flower, suspect it certainly, suspect it and then glide, does that not alter a counting.

A hurt mended stick, a hurt mended cup, a hurt mended article of exceptional relaxation and annoyance, a hurt mended, hurt and mended is so necessary that no mistake is intended.

What is more likely than a roast, nothing really and yet it is never disappointed singularly.

A steady cake, any steady cake is perfect and not plain, any steady cake has a mounting reason and more than that it has singular crusts. A season of more is a season that is instead. A season of many is not more a season than most.

Take no remedy lightly, take no urging intently, take no separation leniently, beware of no lake and no larder.

Burden the cracked wet soaking sack heavily, burden it so that it is an institution in fright and in climate and in the best plan that there can be.

An ordinary color, a color is that strange mixture which makes, which does make which does not make a ripe juice, which does not make a mat.

A work which is a winding a real winding of the cloaking of a relaxing rescue. This which is so cool is not dusting, it is not dirtying in smelling, it could use white water, it could use more extraordinarily and in no solitude altogether. This which is so not winsome and not widened and really not so dipped as dainty and really dainty, very dainty, ordinarily, dainty, a dainty, not in that dainty and dainty. If the time is determined, if it is determined and there is reunion there is reunion with that then outline, then there is in that a piercing shutter, all of a piercing shouter, all of a quite weather, all of a withered exterior, all of that in most violent likely.

An excuse is not dreariness, a single plate is not butter, a single weight is not excitement, a solitary crumbling is not only martial.

A mixed protection, very mixed with the same actual intentional unstrangeness and riding, a single action caused necessarily is not more a sign than a minister.

Seat a knife near a cage and very near a decision and more nearly a timely working cat and scissors. Do this temporarily and make no more mistake in standing. Spread it all and arrange the white place, does this show in the house, does it not show in the green that is not necessary for that color, does it not even show in the explanation and singularly not at all stationary.

SUGAR.

A violent luck and a whole sample and even then quiet.

Water is squeezing, water is almost squeezing on lard. Water, water is a mountain and it is selected and it is so practical that there is no use in money. A mind under is exact and so it is necessary to have a mouth and eye glasses.

A question of sudden rises and more time than awfulness is so easy and shady. There is precisely that noise.

A peck a small piece not privately overseen, not at all not a slice, not at all crestfallen and open, not at all mounting and chaining and evenly surpassing, all the bidding comes to tea.

A separation is not tightly in worsted and sauce, it is so kept well and sectionally.

Put it in the stew, put it to shame. A little slight shadow and a solid fine furnace.

The teasing is tender and trying and thoughtful.

The line which sets sprinkling to be a remedy is beside the best cold.

A puzzle, a monster puzzle, a heavy choking, a neglected Tuesday.

Wet crossing and a likeness, any likeness, a likeness has blisters, it has that and teeth, it has the staggering blindly and a little green, any little green is ordinary.

One, two and one, two, nine, second and five and that.

A blaze, a search in between, a cow, only any wet place, only this tune.

Cut a gas jet uglier and then pierce pierce in between the next and negligence. Choose the rate to pay and pet pet very much. A collection of all around, a signal poison, a lack of languor and more hurts at ease.

A white bird, a colored mine, a mixed orange, a dog.

Cuddling comes in continuing a change.

A piece of separate outstanding rushing is so blind with open delicacy.

A canoe is orderly. A period is solemn. A cow is accepted.

A nice old chain is widening, it is absent, it is laid by.

CRANBERRIES.

Could there not be a sudden date, could there not be in the present settlement of old age pensions, could there not be by a witness, could there be.

Count the chain, cut the grass, silence the noon and murder flies. See the basting undip the chart, see the way the kinds are best seen from the rest, from that and untidy.

Cut the whole space into twenty-four spaces and then and then is there a yellow color, there is but it is smelled, it is then put where it is and nothing stolen.

A remarkable degree of red means that, a remarkable exchange is made.

Climbing altogether in when there is a solid chance of soiling no more than a dirty thing, coloring all of it in steadying is jelly.

Just as it is suffering, just as it is succeeded, just as it is moist so is there no countering.

MILK.

A white egg and a colored pan and a cabbage showing settlement, a constant increase.

A cold in a nose, a single cold nose makes an excuse. Two are more necessary.

All the goods are stolen, all the blisters are in the cup.

Cooking, cooking is the recognition between sudden and nearly sudden very little and all large holes.

A real pint, one that is open and closed and in the middle is so bad.

Tender colds, seen eye holders, all work, the best of change, the meaning, the dark red, all this and bitten, really bitten.

Guessing again and golfing again and the best men, the very best men.

MILK.

Climb up in sight climb in the whole utter needles and a guess a whole guess is hanging. Hanging hanging.

EGGS.

Kind height, kind in the right stomach with a little sudden mill.

Cunning shawl, cunning shawl to be steady.

In white in white handkerchiefs with little dots in a white belt all shadows are singular they are singular and procured and relieved.

No that is not the cows shame and a precocious sound, it is a bite.

Cut up alone the paved way which is harm. Harm is old boat and a likely dash.

APPLE.

Apple plum, carpet steak, seed clam, colored wine, calm seen, cold cream, best shake, potato, potato and no no gold work with pet, a green seen is called bake and change sweet is bready, a little piece a little piece please.

A little piece please. Cane again to the presupposed and ready eucalyptus tree, count out sherry and ripe plates and little corners of a kind of ham. This is use.

TAILS.

Cold pails, cold with joy no joy.

A tiny seat that means meadows and a lapse of cuddles with cheese and nearly bats, all this went messed. The post placed a loud loose sprain. A rest is no better. It is better yet. All the time.

LUNCH.

Luck in loose plaster makes holy gauge and nearly that, nearly more states, more states come in town light kite, blight not white.

A little lunch is a break in skate a little lunch so slimy, a west end of a board line is that which shows a little beneath so that necessity is a silk under wear. That is best wet. It is so natural, and why is there flake, there is flake to explain exhaust.

A real cold hen is nervous is nervous with a towel with a spool with real beads. It is mostly an extra sole nearly all that shaved, shaved with an old mountain, more than that bees more than that dinner and a bunch of likes that is to say the hearts of onions aim less.

Cold coffee with a corn a corn yellow and green mass is a gem.

CUPS.

A single example of excellence is in the meat. A bent stick is surging and might all might is mental. A grand clothes is searching out a candle not that wheatly not that by more than an owl and a path. A ham is proud of cocoanut.

A cup is neglected by being all in size. It is a handle and meadows and sugar any sugar.

A cup is neglected by being full of size. It shows no shade, in come little wood cuts and blessing and nearly not that not with a wild bought in, not at all so polite, not nearly so behind.

Cups crane in. They need a pet oyster, they need it so hoary and nearly choice. The best slam is utter. Nearly be freeze.

Why is a cup a stir and a behave. Why is it so seen.

A cup is readily shaded, it has in between no sense that is to say music, memory, musical memory.

Peanuts blame, a half sand is holey and nearly.

RHUBARB.

Rhubarb is susan not susan not seat in bunch toys not wild and laughable not in little places not in neglect and vegetable not in fold coal age not please.

SINGLE FISH.

Single fish single fish single fish egg-plant single fish sight.

A sweet win and not less noisy than saddle and more ploughing and nearly well painted by little things so.

Please shade it a play. It is necessary and beside the large sort is puff.

Every way oakly, please prune it near. It is so found.

It is not the same.

CAKE.

Cake cast in went to be and needles wine needles are such.

This is today. A can experiment is that which makes a town, makes a town dirty, it is little please. We came back. Two bore, bore what, a mussed ash, ash when there is tin. This meant cake. It was a sign.

Another time there was extra a hat pin sought long and this dark made a display. The result was yellow. A caution, not a caution to be.

It is no use to cause a foolish number. A blanket stretch a cloud, a shame, all that bakery can tease, all that is beginning and yesterday yesterday we had it met. It means some change. No some day.

A little leaf upon a scene an ocean any where there, a bland and likely in the stream a recollection green land. Why white.

CUSTARD.

Custard is this. It has aches, aches when. Not to be. Not to be narrowly. This makes a whole little hill.

It is better than a little thing that has mellow real mellow. It is better than lakes whole lakes, it is better than seeding.

POTATOES.

Real potatoes cut in between.

POTATOES.

In the preparation of cheese, in the preparation of crackers, in the preparation of butter, in it.

ROAST POTATOES.

Roast potatoes for.

ASPARAGUS.

Asparagus in a lean in a lean to hot. This makes it art and it is wet wet weather wet weather wet.

BUTTER.

Boom in boom in, butter. Leave a grain and show it, show it. I spy.

It is a need it is a need that a flower a state flower. It is a need that a state rubber. It is a need that a state rubber is sweet and sight and a swelled stretch. It is a need. It is a need that state rubber.

Wood a supply. Clean little keep a strange, estrange on it.

Make a little white, no and not with pit, pit on in within.

END OF SUMMER.

Little eyelets that have hammer and a check with stripes between a lounge, in wit, in a rested development.

SAUSAGES.

Sausages in between a glass.

There is read butter. A loaf of it is managed. Wake a question. Eat an instant, answer.

A reason for bed is this, that a decline, any decline is poison, poison is a toe a toe extractor, this means a solemn change. Hanging.

No evil is wide, any extra in leaf is so strange and singular a red breast.

CELERY.

Celery tastes tastes where in curled lashes and little bits and mostly in remains.

A green acre is so selfish and so pure and so enlivened.

VEAL.

Very well very well, washing is old, washing is washing.

Cold soup, cold soup clear and particular and a principal a principal question to put into.

VEGETABLE.

What is cut. What is cut by it. What is cut by it in.

It was a cress a crescent a cross and an unequal scream, it was upslanting, it was radiant and reasonable with little ins and red.

News. News capable of glees, cut in shoes, belike under pump of wide chalk, all this combing.

WAY LAY VEGETABLE.

Leaves in grass and mow potatoes, have a skip, hurry you up flutter.

Suppose it is ex a cake suppose it is new mercy and leave charlotte and nervous bed rows. Suppose it is meal. Suppose it is sam.

COOKING.

Alas, alas the pull alas the bell alas the coach in china, alas the little put in leaf alas the wedding butter meat, alas the receptacle, alas the back shape of mussle, mussle and soda.

CHICKEN.

Pheasant and chicken, chicken is a peculiar third.

CHICKEN.

Alas a dirty word, alas a dirty third alas a dirty third, alas a dirty bird.

CHICKEN.

Alas a doubt in case of more go to say what it is cress. What is it. Mean. Potato. Loaves.

CHICKEN.

Stick stick call then, stick stick sticking, sticking with a chicken. Sticking in a extra succession, sticking in.

CHAIN-BOATS.

Chain-boats are merry, are merry blew, blew west, carpet.

PASTRY.

Cutting shade, cool spades and little last beds, make violet, violet when.

CREAM.

In a plank, in a play sole, in a heated red left tree there is shut in specs with salt be where. This makes an eddy. Necessary.

CREAM.

Cream cut. Any where crumb. Left hop chambers.

CUCUMBER.

Not a razor less, not a razor, ridiculous pudding, red and relet put in, rest in a slender go in selecting, rest in, rest in in white widening.

DINNER.

Not a little fit, not a little fit sun sat in shed more mentally.

Let us why, let us why weight, let us why winter chess, let us why way.

Only a moon to soup her, only that in the sell never never be the cocups nice be, shatter it they lay.

Egg ear nuts, look a bout. Shoulder. Let it strange, sold in bell next herds.

It was a time when in the acres in late there was a wheel that shot a burst of land and needless are niggers and a sample sample set of old eaten butterflies with spoons, all of it to be are fled and measure make it, make it, yet all the one in that we see where shall not it set with a left and more so, yes there add when the longer not it shall the best in the way when all be with when shall not for there with see and chest how for another excellent and excellent and easy easy excellent and easy express e c, all to be nice all to be no so. All to be no so no so. All to be not a white old chat churner. Not to be any example of an edible apple in.

DINING.

Dining is west.

EATING.

Eat ting, eating a grand old man said roof and never never re soluble burst, not a near ring not a bewildered neck, not really any such bay.

Is it so a noise to be is it a least remain to rest, is it a so old say to be, is it a leading are been. Is it so, is it so, is it so, is it so is it so is it so.

Eel us eel us with no no pea no pea cool, no pea cool cooler, no pea cooler with a land a land cost in, with a land cost in stretches.

Eating he heat eating he heat it eating, he heat it heat eating. He heat eating.

A little piece of pay of pay owls owls such as pie, bolsters.

Will leap beat, willie well all. The rest rest oxen occasion occasion to be so purred, so purred how.

It was a ham it was a square come well it was a square remain, a square remain not it a bundle, not it a bundle so is a grip, a grip to shed bay leave bay leave draught, bay leave draw cider in low, cider in low and george. George is a mass.

EATING.

It was a shame it was a shame to stare to stare and double and relieve relieve be cut up show as by the elevation of it and out out more in the steady where the come and on and the all the shed and that.

It was a garden and belows belows straight. It was a pea, a pea pour it in its not a succession, not it a simple, not it a so election, election with.

SALAD.

It is a winning cake.

SAUCE.

What is bay labored what is all be section, what is no much. Sauce sam in.

SALMON.

It was a peculiar bin a bin fond in beside.

ORANGE.

Why is a feel oyster an egg stir. Why is it orange centre.

A show at tick and loosen loosen it so to speak sat.

It was an extra leaker with a see spoon, it was an extra licker with a see spoon.

ORANGE.

A type oh oh new new not no not knealer knealer of old show beefsteak, neither neither.

ORANGES.

Build is all right.

ORANGE IN.

Go lack go lack use to her.

Cocoa and clear soup and oranges and oat-meal.

Whist bottom whist close, whist clothes, woodling.

Cocoa and clear soup and oranges and oat-meal.

Pain soup, suppose it is question, suppose it is butter, real is, real is only, only excreate, only excreate a no since.

A no, a no since, a no since when, a no since when since, a no since when since a no since when since, a no since, a no since when since, a no since, a no, a no since a no since, a no since, a no since.

SALAD DRESSING AND AN ARTICHOKE.

Please pale hot, please cover rose, please acre in the red stranger, please butter all the beef-steak with regular feel faces.

SALAD DRESSING AND AN ARTICHOKE.

It was please it was please carriage cup in an ice-cream, in an ice-cream it was too bended bended with scissors and all this time. A whole is inside a part, a part does go away, a hole is red leaf. No choice was where there was and a second and a second.

A CENTRE IN A TABLE.

It was a way a day, this made some sum. Suppose a cod liver a cod liver is an oil, suppose a cod liver oil is tunny, suppose a cod liver oil tunny is pressed suppose a cod liver oil tunny pressed is china and secret with a bestow a bestow reed, a reed to be a reed to be, in a reed to be.

Next to me next to a folder, next to a folder some waiter, next to a foldersome waiter and re letter and read her. Read her with her for less.

ROOMS

Act so that there is no use in a centre. A wide action is not a width. A preparation is given to the ones preparing. They do not eat who mention silver and sweet. There was an occupation.

A whole centre and a border make hanging a way of dressing. This which is not why there is a voice is the remains of an offering. There was no rental.

So the tune which is there has a little piece to play, and the exercise is all there is of a fast. The tender and true that makes no width to hew is the time that there is question to adopt.

To begin the placing there is no wagon. There is no change lighter. It was done. And then the spreading, that was not accomplishing that needed standing and yet the time was not so difficult as they were not all in place. They had no change. They were not respected. They were that, they did it so much in the matter and this showed that that settlement was not condensed. It was spread there. Any change was in the ends of the centre. A heap was heavy. There was no change.

Burnt and behind and lifting a temporary stone and lifting more than a drawer.

The instance of there being more is an instance of more. The shadow is not shining in the way there is a black line. The truth has come. There is a disturbance. Trusting to a baker's boy meant that there would be very much exchanging and anyway what is the use of a covering to a door. There is a use, they are double.

If the centre has the place then there is distribution. That is natural. There is a contradiction and naturally returning there comes to be both sides and the centre. That can be seen from the description.

The author of all that is in there behind the door and that is entering in the morning. Explaining darkening and expecting relating is all of a piece. The stove is bigger. It was of a shape that made no audience bigger if the opening is assumed why should there not be kneeling. Any force which is bestowed on a floor shows rubbing. This is so nice and sweet and yet there comes the change, there comes the time to press more air. This does not mean the same as disappearance.

A little lingering lion and a Chinese chair, all the handsome cheese which is stone, all of it and a choice, a choice of a blotter. If it is difficult to do it one way there is no place of similar trouble. None. The whole arrangement is established. The end of which is that there is a suggestion, a suggestion that there can be a different whiteness to a wall. This was thought.

A page to a corner means that the shame is no greater when the table is longer. A glass is of any height, it is higher, it is simpler and if it were placed there would not be any doubt.

Something that is an erection is that which stands and feeds and silences a tin which is swelling. This makes no diversion that is to say what can please exaltation, that which is cooking.

A shine is that which when covered changes permission. An enclosure blends with the same that is to say there is blending. A blend is that which holds no mice and this is not because of a floor it is because of nothing, it is not in a vision.

A fact is that when the place was replaced all was left that was stored and all was retained that would not satisfy more than another. The question is this, is it possible to suggest more to replace that thing. This question and this perfect denial does make the time change all the time.

The sister was not a mister. Was this a surprise. It was. The conclusion came when there was no arrangement. All the time that there was a question there was a decision. Replacing a casual acquaintance with an ordinary daughter does not make a son.

It happened in a way that the time was perfect and there was a growth of a whole dividing time so that where formerly there was no mistake there was no mistake now. For instance before when there was a separation there was waiting, now when there is separation there is the division between intending and departing. This made no more mixture than there would be if there had been no change.

A little sign of an entrance is the one that made it alike. If it were smaller it was not alike and it was so much smaller that a table was bigger. A table was much bigger, very much bigger. Changing that made nothing bigger, it did not make anything bigger littler, it did not hinder wood from not being used as leather. And this was so charming. Harmony is so essential. Is there pleasure when there is a passage, there is when every room is open. Every room is open when there are not four, there were there and surely there were four, there were two together. There is no resemblance.

A single speed, the reception of table linen, all the wonder of six little spoons, there is no exercise.

The time came when there was a birthday. Every day was no excitement and a birthday was added, it was added on Monday, this made the memory clear, this which was a speech showed the chair in the middle where there was copper.

Alike and a snail, this means Chinamen, it does there is no doubt that to be right is more than perfect there is no doubt and glass is confusing it confuses the substance which was of a color. Then came the time for discrimination, it came then and it was never mentioned it was so triumphant, it showed the whole head that had a hole and should have a hole it showed the resemblance between silver.

Startling a starving husband is not disagreeable. The reason that nothing is hidden is that there is no suggestion of silence. No song is sad. A lesson is of consequence.

Blind and weak and organised and worried and betrothed and resumed and also asked to a fast and always asked to consider and never startled and not at all bloated, this which is no rarer than frequently is not so astonishing when hair brushing is added. There is quiet, there certainly is.

No eye-glasses are rotten, no window is useless and yet if air will not come in there is a speech ready, there always is and there is no dimness, not a bit of it.

All along the tendency to deplore the absence of more has not been authorised. It comes to mean that with burning there is that pleasant state of stupefication. Then there is a way of earning a living. Who is a man.

A silence is not indicated by any motion, less is indicated by a motion, more is not indicated it is enthralled. So sullen and so low, so much resignation, so much refusal and so much place for a lower and an upper, so much and yet more silence, why is not sleeping a feat why is it not and when is there some discharge when. There never is.

If comparing a piece that is a size that is recognised as not a size but a piece, comparing a piece with what is not recognised but what is used as it is held by holding, comparing these two comes to be repeated. Suppose they are put together, suppose that there is an interruption, supposing that beginning again they are not changed as to position, suppose all this and suppose that any five two of whom are not separating suppose that the five are not consumed. Is there an exchange, is there a resemblance to the sky which is admitted to be there and the stars which can be seen. Is there. That was a question. There was no certainty. Fitting a failing meant that any two were indifferent and yet they were all connecting that, they were all connecting that consideration. This did not determine rejoining a letter. This did not make letters smaller. It did.

The stamp that is not only torn but also fitting is not any symbol. It suggests nothing. A sack that has no opening suggests more and the loss is not commensurate. The season gliding and the torn hangings receiving mending all this shows an example, it shows the force of sacrifice and likeness and disaster and a reason.

The time when there is not the question is only seen when there is a shower. Any little thing is water.

There was a whole collection made. A damp cloth, an oyster, a single mirror, a manikin, a student, a silent star, a single spark, a little movement and the bed is made. This shows the disorder, it does, it shows more likeness than anything else, it shows the single mind that directs an apple. All the coats have a different shape, that does not mean that they differ in color, it means a union between use and exercise and a horse.

A plain hill, one is not that which is not white and red and green, a plain hill makes no sunshine, it shows that without a disturber. So the shape is there and the color and the outline and the miserable centre, it is not very likely that there is a centre, a hill is a hill and no hill is contained in a pink tender descender.

A can containing a curtain is a solid sentimental usage. The trouble in both eyes does not come from the same symmetrical carpet, it comes from there being no more disturbance than in little paper. This does show the teeth, it shows color.

A measure is that which put up so that it shows the length has a steel construction. Tidiness is not delicacy, it does not destroy the whole piece, certainly not it has been measured and nothing has been cut off and even if that has been lost there is a name, no name is signed and left over, not any space is fitted so that moving about is plentiful. Why is there so much resignation in a package, why is there rain, all the same the chance has come, there is no bell to ring.

A package and a filter and even a funnel, all this together makes a scene and supposing the question arises is hair curly, is it dark and dusty, supposing that question arises, is brushing necessary, is it, the whole special suddenness commences then, there is no delusion.

A cape is a cover, a cape is not a cover in summer, a cape is a cover and the regulation is that there is no such weather. A cape is not always a cover, a cape is not a cover when there is another, there is always something in that thing in establishing a disposition to put wetting where it will not do more harm. There is always that disposition and in a way there is some use in not mentioning changing and in establishing the temperature, there is some use in it as establishing all that lives dimmer freer and there is no dinner in the middle of anything. There is no such thing.

Why is a pale white not paler than blue, why is a connection made by a stove, why is the example which is mentioned not shown to be the same, why is there no adjustment between the place and the separate attention. Why is there a choice in gamboling. Why is there no necessary dull stable, why is there a single piece of any color, why is there that sensible silence. Why is there the resistance in a mixture, why is there no poster, why is there that in the window, why is there no suggester, why is there no window, why is there no oyster closer. Why is there a circular diminisher, why is there a bather, why is there no scraper, why is there a dinner, why is there a bell ringer, why is there a duster, why is there a section of a similar resemblance, why is there that scissor.

South, south which is a wind is not rain, does silence choke speech or does it not.

Lying in a conundrum, lying so makes the springs restless, lying so is a reduction, not lying so is arrangeable.

Releasing the oldest auction that is the pleasing some still renewing.

Giving it away, not giving it away, is there any difference. Giving it away. Not giving it away.

Almost very likely there is no seduction, almost very likely there is no stream, certainly very likely the height is penetrated, certainly certainly the target is cleaned. Come to sit, come to refuse, come to surround, come slowly and age is not lessening. The time which showed that was when there was no eclipse. All the time that resenting was removal all that time there was breadth. No breath is shadowed, no breath is paintaking and yet certainly what could be the use of paper, paper shows no disorder, it shows no desertion.

Why is there a difference between one window and another, why is there a difference, because the curtain is shorter. There is no distaste in beefsteak or in plums or in gallons of milk water, there is no defiance in original piling up over a roof, there is no daylight in the evening, there is none there empty.

A tribune, a tribune does not mean paper, it means nothing more than cake, it means more sugar, it shows the state of lengthening any nose. The last spice is that which shows the whole evening spent in that sleep, it shows so that walking is an alleviation, and yet this astonishes everybody the distance is so sprightly. In all the time there are three days, those are not passed uselessly. Any little thing is a change that is if nothing is wasted in that cellar. All the rest of the chairs are established.

A success, a success is alright when there are there rooms and no vacancies, a success is alright when there is a package, success is alright anyway and any curtain is wholesale. A curtain diminishes and an ample space shows varnish.

One taste one tack, one taste one bottle, one taste one fish, one taste one barometer. This shows no distinguishing sign when there is a store.

Any smile is stern and any coat is a sample. Is there any use in changing more doors than there are committees. This question is so often asked that squares show that they are blotters. It is so very agreeable to hear a voice and to see all the signs of that expression.

Cadences, real cadences, real cadences and a quiet color. Careful and curved, cake and sober, all accounts and mixture, a guess at anything is righteous, should there be a call there would be a voice.

A line in life, a single line and a stairway, a rigid cook, no cook and no equator, all the same there is higher than that another evasion. Did that mean shame, it meant memory. Looking into a place that was hanging and was visible looking into this place and seeing a chair did that mean relief, it did, it certainly did not cause constipation and yet there is a melody that has white for a tune when there is straw color. This shows no face.

Star-light, what is star-light, star-light is a little light that is not always mentioned with the sun, it is mentioned with the moon and the sun, it is mixed up with the rest of the time.

Why is the name changed. The name is changed because in the little space there is a tree, in some space there are no trees, in every space there is a hint of more, all this causes the decision.

Why is there education, there is education because the two tables which are folding are not tied together with a ribbon, string is used and string being used there is a necessity for another one and another one not being used to hearing shows no ordinary use of any evening and yet there is no disgrace in looking, none at all. This came to separate when there was simple selection of an entire pre-occupation.

A curtain, a curtain which is fastened discloses mourning, this does not mean sparrows or elocution or even a whole preparation, it means that there are ears and very often much more altogether.

Climate, climate is not southern, a little glass, a bright winter, a strange supper an elastic tumbler, all this shows that the back is furnished and red which is red is a dark color. An example of this is fifteen years and a separation of regret.

China is not down when there are plates, lights are not ponderous and incalculable.

Currents, currents are not in the air and on the floor and in the door and behind it first. Currents do not show it plainer. This which is mastered has so thin a space to build it all that there is plenty of room and yet is it quarreling, it is not and the insistence is marked. A change is in a current and there is no habitable exercise.

A religion, almost a religion, any religion, a quintal in religion, a relying and a surface and a service in indecision and a creature and a question and a syllable in answer and more counting and no quarrel and a single scientific statement and no darkness and no question and an earned administration and a single set of sisters and an outline and no blisters and the section seeing yellow and the centre having spelling and no solitude and no quaintness and yet solid quite so solid and the single surface centred and the question in the placard and the singularity, is there a singularity, and the singularity, why is there a question and the singularity why is the surface outrageous, why is it beautiful why is it not when there is no doubt, why is anything vacant, why is not disturbing a centre no virtue, why is it when it is and why is it when it is and there is no doubt, there is no doubt that the singularity shows.

A climate, a single climate, all the time there is a single climate, any time there is a doubt, any time there is music that is to question more and more and there is no politeness, there is hardly any ordeal and certainly there is no tablecloth.

This is a sound and obligingness more obligingness leads to a harmony in hesitation.

A lake a single lake which is a pond and a little water any water which is an ant and no burning, not any burning, all this is sudden.

A canister that is the remains of furniture and a looking-glass and a bed-room and a larger size, all the stand is shouted and what is ancient is practical. Should the resemblance be so that any little cover is copied, should it be so that yards are measured, should it be so and there be a sin, should it be so then certainly a room is big enough when it is so empty and the corners are gathered together.

The change is mercenary that settles whitening the coloring and serving dishes where there is metal and making yellow any yellow every color in a shade which is expressed in a tray. This is a monster and awkward quite awkward and the little design which is flowered which is not strange and yet has visible writing, this is not shown all the time but at once, after that it rests where it is and where it is in place. No change is not needed. That does show design.

Excellent, more excellence is borrowing and slanting very slanting is light and secret and a recitation and emigration. Certainly shoals are shallow and nonsense more nonsense is sullen. Very little cake is water, very little cake has that escape.

Sugar any sugar, anger every anger, lover sermon lover, centre no distractor, all order is in a measure.

Left over to be a lamp light, left over in victory, left over in saving, all this and negligence and bent wood and more even much more is not so exact as a pen and a turtle and even, certainly, and even a piece of the same experience as more.

To consider a lecture, to consider it well is so anxious and so much a charity and really supposing there is grain and if a stubble every stubble is urgent, will there not be a chance of legality. The sound is sickened and the price is purchased and golden what is golden, a clergyman, a single tax, a currency and an inner chamber.

Checking an emigration, checking it by smiling and certainly by the same satisfactory stretch of hands that have more use for it than nothing, and mildly not mildly a correction, not mildly even a circumstance and a sweetness and a serenity. Powder, that has no color, if it did have would it be white.

A whole soldier any whole soldier has no more detail than any case of measles.

A bridge a very small bridge in a location and thunder, any thunder, this is the capture of reversible sizing and more indeed more can be cautious. This which makes monotony careless makes it likely that there is an exchange in principle and more than that, change in organization.

This cloud does change with the movements of the moon and the narrow the quite narrow suggestion of the building. It does and then when it is settled and no sounds differ then comes the moment when cheerfulness is so assured that there is an occasion.

A plain lap, any plain lap shows that sign, it shows that there is not so much extension as there would be if there were more choice in everything. And why complain of more, why complain of very much more. Why complain at all when it is all arranged that as there is no more opportunity and no more appeal and not even any more clinching that certainly now some time has come.

A window has another spelling, it has "f" all together, it lacks no more then and this is rain, this may even be something else, at any rate there is no dedication in splendor. There is a turn of the stranger.

Catholic to be turned is to venture on youth and a section of debate, it even means that no class where each one over fifty is regular is so stationary that there are invitations.

A curving example makes righteous finger-nails. This is the only object in secretion and speech.

To being the same four are no more than were taller. The rest had a big chair and a surveyance a cold accumulation of nausea, and even more than that, they had a disappointment.

Nothing aiming is a flower, if flowers are abundant then they are lilac, if they are not they are white in the centre.

Dance a clean dream and an extravagant turn up, secure the steady rights and translate more than translate the authority, show the choice and make no more mistakes than yesterday.

This means clearness, it means a regular notion of exercise, it means more than that, it means liking counting, it means more than that, it does not mean exchanging a line.

Why is there more craving than there is in a mountain. This does not seem strange to one, it does not seem strange to an echo and more surely is in there not being a habit. Why is there so much useless suffering. Why is there.

Any wet weather means an open window, what is attaching eating, anything that is violent and cooking and shows weather is the same in the end and why is there more use in something than in all that.

The cases are made and books, back books are used to secure tears and church. They are even used to exchange black slippers. They can not be mended with wax. They show no need of any such occasion.

A willow and no window, a wide place stranger, a wideness makes an active center.

The sight of no pussy cat is so different that a tobacco zone is white and cream.

A lilac, all a lilac and no mention of butter, not even bread and butter, no butter and no occasion, not even a silent resemblance, not more care than just enough haughty.

A safe weight is that which when it pleases is hanging. A safer weight is one more naughty in a spectacle. The best game is that which is shiny and scratching. Please a pease and a cracker and a wretched use of summer.

Surprise, the only surprise has no occasion. It is an ingredient and the section the whole section is one season.

A pecking which is petting and no worse than in the same morning is not the only way to be continuous often.

A light in the moon the only light is on Sunday. What was the sensible decision. The sensible decision was that notwithstanding many declarations and more music, not even notwithstanding the choice and a torch and a collection, notwithstanding the celebrating hat and a vacation and even more noise than cutting, notwithstanding Europe and Asia and being overbearing, not even notwithstanding an elephant and a strict occasion, not even withstanding more cultivation and some seasoning, not even with drowning and with the ocean being encircling, not even with more likeness and any cloud, not even with terrific sacrifice of pedestrianism and a special resolution, not even more likely to be pleasing. The care with which the rain is wrong and the green is wrong and the white is wrong, the care with which there is a chair and plenty of breathing. The care with which there is incredible justice and likeness, all this makes a magnificent asparagus, and also a fountain.

A CATALOG OF SELECTED

DOVER BOOKS

IN ALL FIELDS OF INTEREST

A CATALOG OF SELECTED DOVER BOOKS IN ALL FIELDS OF INTEREST

CONCERNING THE SPIRITUAL IN ART, Wassily Kandinsky. Pioneering work by father of abstract art. Thoughts on color theory, nature of art. Analysis of earlier masters. 12 illustrations. 80pp. of text. 5⅜ x 8½. 23411-8

ANIMALS: 1,419 Copyright-Free Illustrations of Mammals, Birds, Fish, Insects, etc., Jim Harter (ed.). Clear wood engravings present, in extremely lifelike poses, over 1,000 species of animals. One of the most extensive pictorial sourcebooks of its kind. Captions. Index. 284pp. 9 x 12. 23766-4

CELTIC ART: The Methods of Construction, George Bain. Simple geometric techniques for making Celtic interlacements, spirals, Kells-type initials, animals, humans, etc. Over 500 illustrations. 160pp. 9 x 12. (Available in U.S. only.) 22923-8

AN ATLAS OF ANATOMY FOR ARTISTS, Fritz Schider. Most thorough reference work on art anatomy in the world. Hundreds of illustrations, including selections from works by Vesalius, Leonardo, Goya, Ingres, Michelangelo, others. 593 illustrations. 192pp. 7⅛ x 10¼. 20241-0

CELTIC HAND STROKE-BY-STROKE (Irish Half-Uncial from "The Book of Kells"): An Arthur Baker Calligraphy Manual, Arthur Baker. Complete guide to creating each letter of the alphabet in distinctive Celtic manner. Covers hand position, strokes, pens, inks, paper, more. Illustrated. 48pp. 8¼ x 11. 24336-2

EASY ORIGAMI, John Montroll. Charming collection of 32 projects (hat, cup, pelican, piano, swan, many more) specially designed for the novice origami hobbyist. Clearly illustrated easy-to-follow instructions insure that even beginning papercrafters will achieve successful results. 48pp. 8¼ x 11. 27298-2

THE COMPLETE BOOK OF BIRDHOUSE CONSTRUCTION FOR WOODWORKERS, Scott D. Campbell. Detailed instructions, illustrations, tables. Also data on bird habitat and instinct patterns. Bibliography. 3 tables. 63 illustrations in 15 figures. 48pp. 5¼ x 8½. 24407-5

BLOOMINGDALE'S ILLUSTRATED 1886 CATALOG: Fashions, Dry Goods and Housewares, Bloomingdale Brothers. Famed merchants' extremely rare catalog depicting about 1,700 products: clothing, housewares, firearms, dry goods, jewelry, more. Invaluable for dating, identifying vintage items. Also, copyright-free graphics for artists, designers. Co-published with Henry Ford Museum & Greenfield Village. 160pp. 8¼ x 11. 25780-0

HISTORIC COSTUME IN PICTURES, Braun & Schneider. Over 1,450 costumed figures in clearly detailed engravings–from dawn of civilization to end of 19th century. Captions. Many folk costumes. 256pp. 8⅜ x 11¾. 23150-X

THE CLARINET AND CLARINET PLAYING, David Pino. Lively, comprehensive work features suggestions about technique, musicianship, and musical interpretation, as well as guidelines for teaching, making your own reeds, and preparing for public performance. Includes an intriguing look at clarinet history. "A godsend," *The Clarinet,* Journal of the International Clarinet Society. Appendixes. 7 illus. 320pp. 5⅜ x 8½. 40270-3

HOLLYWOOD GLAMOR PORTRAITS, John Kobal (ed.). 145 photos from 1926-49. Harlow, Gable, Bogart, Bacall; 94 stars in all. Full background on photographers, technical aspects. 160pp. 8⅜ x 11¼. 23352-9

THE ANNOTATED CASEY AT THE BAT: A Collection of Ballads about the Mighty Casey/Third, Revised Edition, Martin Gardner (ed.). Amusing sequels and parodies of one of America's best-loved poems: Casey's Revenge, Why Casey Whiffed, Casey's Sister at the Bat, others. 256pp. 5⅜ x 8½. 28598-7

THE RAVEN AND OTHER FAVORITE POEMS, Edgar Allan Poe. Over 40 of the author's most memorable poems: "The Bells," "Ulalume," "Israfel," "To Helen," "The Conqueror Worm," "Eldorado," "Annabel Lee," many more. Alphabetic lists of titles and first lines. 64pp. 5³⁄₁₆ x 8¼. 26685-0

PERSONAL MEMOIRS OF U. S. GRANT, Ulysses Simpson Grant. Intelligent, deeply moving firsthand account of Civil War campaigns, considered by many the finest military memoirs ever written. Includes letters, historic photographs, maps and more. 528pp. 6⅛ x 9¼. 28587-1

ANCIENT EGYPTIAN MATERIALS AND INDUSTRIES, A. Lucas and J. Harris. Fascinating, comprehensive, thoroughly documented text describes this ancient civilization's vast resources and the processes that incorporated them in daily life, including the use of animal products, building materials, cosmetics, perfumes and incense, fibers, glazed ware, glass and its manufacture, materials used in the mummification process, and much more. 544pp. 6⅛ x 9¼. (Available in U.S. only.) 40446-3

RUSSIAN STORIES/RUSSKIE RASSKAZY: A Dual-Language Book, edited by Gleb Struve. Twelve tales by such masters as Chekhov, Tolstoy, Dostoevsky, Pushkin, others. Excellent word-for-word English translations on facing pages, plus teaching and study aids, Russian/English vocabulary, biographical/critical introductions, more. 416pp. 5⅜ x 8½. 26244-8

PHILADELPHIA THEN AND NOW: 60 Sites Photographed in the Past and Present, Kenneth Finkel and Susan Oyama. Rare photographs of City Hall, Logan Square, Independence Hall, Betsy Ross House, other landmarks juxtaposed with contemporary views. Captures changing face of historic city. Introduction. Captions. 128pp. 8¼ x 11. 25790-8

AIA ARCHITECTURAL GUIDE TO NASSAU AND SUFFOLK COUNTIES, LONG ISLAND, The American Institute of Architects, Long Island Chapter, and the Society for the Preservation of Long Island Antiquities. Comprehensive, well-researched and generously illustrated volume brings to life over three centuries of Long Island's great architectural heritage. More than 240 photographs with authoritative, extensively detailed captions. 176pp. 8¼ x 11. 26946-9

NORTH AMERICAN INDIAN LIFE: Customs and Traditions of 23 Tribes, Elsie Clews Parsons (ed.). 27 fictionalized essays by noted anthropologists examine religion, customs, government, additional facets of life among the Winnebago, Crow, Zuni, Eskimo, other tribes. 480pp. 6⅛ x 9¼. 27377-6

FRANK LLOYD WRIGHT'S DANA HOUSE, Donald Hoffmann. Pictorial essay of residential masterpiece with over 160 interior and exterior photos, plans, elevations, sketches and studies. 128pp. 9¼ x 10¾. 29120-0

THE MALE AND FEMALE FIGURE IN MOTION: 60 Classic Photographic Sequences, Eadweard Muybridge. 60 true-action photographs of men and women walking, running, climbing, bending, turning, etc., reproduced from rare 19th-century masterpiece. vi + 121pp. 9 x 12. 24745-7

1001 QUESTIONS ANSWERED ABOUT THE SEASHORE, N. J. Berrill and Jacquelyn Berrill. Queries answered about dolphins, sea snails, sponges, starfish, fishes, shore birds, many others. Covers appearance, breeding, growth, feeding, much more. 305pp. 5¼ x 8¼. 23366-9

ATTRACTING BIRDS TO YOUR YARD, William J. Weber. Easy-to-follow guide offers advice on how to attract the greatest diversity of birds: birdhouses, feeders, water and waterers, much more. 96pp. $5\frac{3}{16}$ x 8¼. 28927-3

MEDICINAL AND OTHER USES OF NORTH AMERICAN PLANTS: A Historical Survey with Special Reference to the Eastern Indian Tribes, Charlotte Erichsen-Brown. Chronological historical citations document 500 years of usage of plants, trees, shrubs native to eastern Canada, northeastern U.S. Also complete identifying information. 343 illustrations. 544pp. 6½ x 9¼. 25951-X

STORYBOOK MAZES, Dave Phillips. 23 stories and mazes on two-page spreads: Wizard of Oz, Treasure Island, Robin Hood, etc. Solutions. 64pp. 8¼ x 11. 23628-5

AMERICAN NEGRO SONGS: 230 Folk Songs and Spirituals, Religious and Secular, John W. Work. This authoritative study traces the African influences of songs sung and played by black Americans at work, in church, and as entertainment. The author discusses the lyric significance of such songs as "Swing Low, Sweet Chariot," "John Henry," and others and offers the words and music for 230 songs. Bibliography. Index of Song Titles. 272pp. 6½ x 9¼. 40271-1

MOVIE-STAR PORTRAITS OF THE FORTIES, John Kobal (ed.). 163 glamor, studio photos of 106 stars of the 1940s: Rita Hayworth, Ava Gardner, Marlon Brando, Clark Gable, many more. 176pp. 8⅜ x 11¼. 23546-7

BENCHLEY LOST AND FOUND, Robert Benchley. Finest humor from early 30s, about pet peeves, child psychologists, post office and others. Mostly unavailable elsewhere. 73 illustrations by Peter Arno and others. 183pp. 5⅜ x 8½. 22410-4

YEKL and THE IMPORTED BRIDEGROOM AND OTHER STORIES OF YIDDISH NEW YORK, Abraham Cahan. Film Hester Street based on *Yekl* (1896). Novel, other stories among first about Jewish immigrants on N.Y.'s East Side. 240pp. 5⅜ x 8½. 22427-9

SELECTED POEMS, Walt Whitman. Generous sampling from *Leaves of Grass*. Twenty-four poems include "I Hear America Singing," "Song of the Open Road," "I Sing the Body Electric," "When Lilacs Last in the Dooryard Bloom'd," "O Captain! My Captain!"–all reprinted from an authoritative edition. Lists of titles and first lines. 128pp. $5\frac{3}{16}$ x 8¼. 26878-0

THE BEST TALES OF HOFFMANN, E. T. A. Hoffmann. 10 of Hoffmann's most important stories: "Nutcracker and the King of Mice," "The Golden Flowerpot," etc. 458pp. 5⅜ x 8½. 21793-0

FROM FETISH TO GOD IN ANCIENT EGYPT, E. A. Wallis Budge. Rich detailed survey of Egyptian conception of "God" and gods, magic, cult of animals, Osiris, more. Also, superb English translations of hymns and legends. 240 illustrations. 545pp. 5⅜ x 8½. 25803-3

FRENCH STORIES/CONTES FRANÇAIS: A Dual-Language Book, Wallace Fowlie. Ten stories by French masters, Voltaire to Camus: "Micromegas" by Voltaire; "The Atheist's Mass" by Balzac; "Minuet" by de Maupassant; "The Guest" by Camus, six more. Excellent English translations on facing pages. Also French-English vocabulary list, exercises, more. 352pp. 5⅜ x 8½. 26443-2

CHICAGO AT THE TURN OF THE CENTURY IN PHOTOGRAPHS: 122 Historic Views from the Collections of the Chicago Historical Society, Larry A. Viskochil. Rare large-format prints offer detailed views of City Hall, State Street, the Loop, Hull House, Union Station, many other landmarks, circa 1904-1913. Introduction. Captions. Maps. 144pp. 9⅜ x 12¼. 24656-6

OLD BROOKLYN IN EARLY PHOTOGRAPHS, 1865-1929, William Lee Younger. Luna Park, Gravesend race track, construction of Grand Army Plaza, moving of Hotel Brighton, etc. 157 previously unpublished photographs. 165pp. 8⅞ x 11¾. 23587-4

THE MYTHS OF THE NORTH AMERICAN INDIANS, Lewis Spence. Rich anthology of the myths and legends of the Algonquins, Iroquois, Pawnees and Sioux, prefaced by an extensive historical and ethnological commentary. 36 illustrations. 480pp. 5⅜ x 8½. 25967-6

AN ENCYCLOPEDIA OF BATTLES: Accounts of Over 1,560 Battles from 1479 B.C. to the Present, David Eggenberger. Essential details of every major battle in recorded history from the first battle of Megiddo in 1479 B.C. to Grenada in 1984. List of Battle Maps. New Appendix covering the years 1967-1984. Index. 99 illustrations. 544pp. 6½ x 9¼. 24913-1

SAILING ALONE AROUND THE WORLD, Captain Joshua Slocum. First man to sail around the world, alone, in small boat. One of great feats of seamanship told in delightful manner. 67 illustrations. 294pp. 5⅜ x 8½. 20326-3

ANARCHISM AND OTHER ESSAYS, Emma Goldman. Powerful, penetrating, prophetic essays on direct action, role of minorities, prison reform, puritan hypocrisy, violence, etc. 271pp. 5⅜ x 8½. 22484-8

MYTHS OF THE HINDUS AND BUDDHISTS, Ananda K. Coomaraswamy and Sister Nivedita. Great stories of the epics; deeds of Krishna, Shiva, taken from puranas, Vedas, folk tales; etc. 32 illustrations. 400pp. 5⅜ x 8½. 21759-0

THE TRAUMA OF BIRTH, Otto Rank. Rank's controversial thesis that anxiety neurosis is caused by profound psychological trauma which occurs at birth. 256pp. 5⅜ x 8½. 27974-X

A THEOLOGICO-POLITICAL TREATISE, Benedict Spinoza. Also contains unfinished Political Treatise. Great classic on religious liberty, theory of government on common consent. R. Elwes translation. Total of 421pp. 5⅜ x 8½. 20249-6

MY BONDAGE AND MY FREEDOM, Frederick Douglass. Born a slave, Douglass became outspoken force in antislavery movement. The best of Douglass' autobiographies. Graphic description of slave life. 464pp. 5⅜ x 8½. 22457-0

FOLLOWING THE EQUATOR: A Journey Around the World, Mark Twain. Fascinating humorous account of 1897 voyage to Hawaii, Australia, India, New Zealand, etc. Ironic, bemused reports on peoples, customs, climate, flora and fauna, politics, much more. 197 illustrations. 720pp. 5⅜ x 8½. 26113-1

THE PEOPLE CALLED SHAKERS, Edward D. Andrews. Definitive study of Shakers: origins, beliefs, practices, dances, social organization, furniture and crafts, etc. 33 illustrations. 351pp. 5⅜ x 8½. 21081-2

THE MYTHS OF GREECE AND ROME, H. A. Guerber. A classic of mythology, generously illustrated, long prized for its simple, graphic, accurate retelling of the principal myths of Greece and Rome, and for its commentary on their origins and significance. With 64 illustrations by Michelangelo, Raphael, Titian, Rubens, Canova, Bernini and others. 480pp. 5⅜ x 8½. 27584-1

PSYCHOLOGY OF MUSIC, Carl E. Seashore. Classic work discusses music as a medium from psychological viewpoint. Clear treatment of physical acoustics, auditory apparatus, sound perception, development of musical skills, nature of musical feeling, host of other topics. 88 figures. 408pp. 5⅜ x 8½. 21851-1

THE PHILOSOPHY OF HISTORY, Georg W. Hegel. Great classic of Western thought develops concept that history is not chance but rational process, the evolution of freedom. 457pp. 5⅜ x 8½. 20112-0

THE BOOK OF TEA, Kakuzo Okakura. Minor classic of the Orient: entertaining, charming explanation, interpretation of traditional Japanese culture in terms of tea ceremony. 94pp. 5⅜ x 8½. 20070-1

LIFE IN ANCIENT EGYPT, Adolf Erman. Fullest, most thorough, detailed older account with much not in more recent books, domestic life, religion, magic, medicine, commerce, much more. Many illustrations reproduce tomb paintings, carvings, hieroglyphs, etc. 597pp. 5⅜ x 8½. 22632-8

SUNDIALS, Their Theory and Construction, Albert Waugh. Far and away the best, most thorough coverage of ideas, mathematics concerned, types, construction, adjusting anywhere. Simple, nontechnical treatment allows even children to build several of these dials. Over 100 illustrations. 230pp. 5⅜ x 8½. 22947-5

THEORETICAL HYDRODYNAMICS, L. M. Milne-Thomson. Classic exposition of the mathematical theory of fluid motion, applicable to both hydrodynamics and aerodynamics. Over 600 exercises. 768pp. 6⅛ x 9¼. 68970-0

SONGS OF EXPERIENCE: Facsimile Reproduction with 26 Plates in Full Color, William Blake. 26 full-color plates from a rare 1826 edition. Includes "The Tyger," "London," "Holy Thursday," and other poems. Printed text of poems. 48pp. 5¼ x 7. 24636-1

OLD-TIME VIGNETTES IN FULL COLOR, Carol Belanger Grafton (ed.). Over 390 charming, often sentimental illustrations, selected from archives of Victorian graphics–pretty women posing, children playing, food, flowers, kittens and puppies, smiling cherubs, birds and butterflies, much more. All copyright-free. 48pp. 9¼ x 12¼. 27269-9

ANATOMY: A Complete Guide for Artists, Joseph Sheppard. A master of figure drawing shows artists how to render human anatomy convincingly. Over 460 illustrations. 224pp. 8⅜ x 11¼. 27279-6

MEDIEVAL CALLIGRAPHY: Its History and Technique, Marc Drogin. Spirited history, comprehensive instruction manual covers 13 styles (ca. 4th century through 15th). Excellent photographs; directions for duplicating medieval techniques with modern tools. 224pp. 8⅜ x 11¼. 26142-5

DRIED FLOWERS: How to Prepare Them, Sarah Whitlock and Martha Rankin. Complete instructions on how to use silica gel, meal and borax, perlite aggregate, sand and borax, glycerine and water to create attractive permanent flower arrangements. 12 illustrations. 32pp. 5⅜ x 8½. 21802-3

EASY-TO-MAKE BIRD FEEDERS FOR WOODWORKERS, Scott D. Campbell. Detailed, simple-to-use guide for designing, constructing, caring for and using feeders. Text, illustrations for 12 classic and contemporary designs. 96pp. 5⅜ x 8½. 25847-5

SCOTTISH WONDER TALES FROM MYTH AND LEGEND, Donald A. Mackenzie. 16 lively tales tell of giants rumbling down mountainsides, of a magic wand that turns stone pillars into warriors, of gods and goddesses, evil hags, powerful forces and more. 240pp. 5⅜ x 8½. 29677-6

THE HISTORY OF UNDERCLOTHES, C. Willett Cunnington and Phyllis Cunnington. Fascinating, well-documented survey covering six centuries of English undergarments, enhanced with over 100 illustrations: 12th-century laced-up bodice, footed long drawers (1795), 19th-century bustles, 19th-century corsets for men, Victorian "bust improvers," much more. 272pp. 5⅝ x 8¼. 27124-2

ARTS AND CRAFTS FURNITURE: The Complete Brooks Catalog of 1912, Brooks Manufacturing Co. Photos and detailed descriptions of more than 150 now very collectible furniture designs from the Arts and Crafts movement depict davenports, settees, buffets, desks, tables, chairs, bedsteads, dressers and more, all built of solid, quarter-sawed oak. Invaluable for students and enthusiasts of antiques, Americana and the decorative arts. 80pp. 6½ x 9¼. 27471-3

WILBUR AND ORVILLE: A Biography of the Wright Brothers, Fred Howard. Definitive, crisply written study tells the full story of the brothers' lives and work. A vividly written biography, unparalleled in scope and color, that also captures the spirit of an extraordinary era. 560pp. 6⅛ x 9¼. 40297-5

THE ARTS OF THE SAILOR: Knotting, Splicing and Ropework, Hervey Garrett Smith. Indispensable shipboard reference covers tools, basic knots and useful hitches; handsewing and canvas work, more. Over 100 illustrations. Delightful reading for sea lovers. 256pp. 5⅜ x 8½. 26440-8

FRANK LLOYD WRIGHT'S FALLINGWATER: The House and Its History, Second, Revised Edition, Donald Hoffmann. A total revision–both in text and illustrations–of the standard document on Fallingwater, the boldest, most personal architectural statement of Wright's mature years, updated with valuable new material from the recently opened Frank Lloyd Wright Archives. "Fascinating"–*The New York Times*. 116 illustrations. 128pp. 9¼ x 10¾. 27430-6

PHOTOGRAPHIC SKETCHBOOK OF THE CIVIL WAR, Alexander Gardner. 100 photos taken on field during the Civil War. Famous shots of Manassas Harper's Ferry, Lincoln, Richmond, slave pens, etc. 244pp. 10⅝ x 8¼. 22731-6

FIVE ACRES AND INDEPENDENCE, Maurice G. Kains. Great back-to-the-land classic explains basics of self-sufficient farming. The one book to get. 95 illustrations. 397pp. 5⅜ x 8½. 20974-1

SONGS OF EASTERN BIRDS, Dr. Donald J. Borror. Songs and calls of 60 species most common to eastern U.S.: warblers, woodpeckers, flycatchers, thrushes, larks, many more in high-quality recording. Cassette and manual 99912-2

A MODERN HERBAL, Margaret Grieve. Much the fullest, most exact, most useful compilation of herbal material. Gigantic alphabetical encyclopedia, from aconite to zedoary, gives botanical information, medical properties, folklore, economic uses, much else. Indispensable to serious reader. 161 illustrations. 888pp. 6½ x 9¼. 2-vol. set. (Available in U.S. only.) Vol. I: 22798-7
Vol. II: 22799-5

HIDDEN TREASURE MAZE BOOK, Dave Phillips. Solve 34 challenging mazes accompanied by heroic tales of adventure. Evil dragons, people-eating plants, blood-thirsty giants, many more dangerous adversaries lurk at every twist and turn. 34 mazes, stories, solutions. 48pp. 8¼ x 11. 24566-7

LETTERS OF W. A. MOZART, Wolfgang A. Mozart. Remarkable letters show bawdy wit, humor, imagination, musical insights, contemporary musical world; includes some letters from Leopold Mozart. 276pp. 5⅜ x 8½. 22859-2

BASIC PRINCIPLES OF CLASSICAL BALLET, Agrippina Vaganova. Great Russian theoretician, teacher explains methods for teaching classical ballet. 118 illustrations. 175pp. 5⅜ x 8½. 22036-2

THE JUMPING FROG, Mark Twain. Revenge edition. The original story of The Celebrated Jumping Frog of Calaveras County, a hapless French translation, and Twain's hilarious "retranslation" from the French. 12 illustrations. 66pp. 5⅜ x 8½. 22686-7

BEST REMEMBERED POEMS, Martin Gardner (ed.). The 126 poems in this superb collection of 19th- and 20th-century British and American verse range from Shelley's "To a Skylark" to the impassioned "Renascence" of Edna St. Vincent Millay and to Edward Lear's whimsical "The Owl and the Pussycat." 224pp. 5⅜ x 8½. 27165-X

COMPLETE SONNETS, William Shakespeare. Over 150 exquisite poems deal with love, friendship, the tyranny of time, beauty's evanescence, death and other themes in language of remarkable power, precision and beauty. Glossary of archaic terms. 80pp. 5$\frac{3}{16}$ x 8¼. 26686-9

THE BATTLES THAT CHANGED HISTORY, Fletcher Pratt. Eminent historian profiles 16 crucial conflicts, ancient to modern, that changed the course of civilization. 352pp. 5⅜ x 8½. 41129-X

THE WIT AND HUMOR OF OSCAR WILDE, Alvin Redman (ed.). More than 1,000 ripostes, paradoxes, wisecracks: Work is the curse of the drinking classes; I can resist everything except temptation; etc. 258pp. 5⅜ x 8½. 20602-5

SHAKESPEARE LEXICON AND QUOTATION DICTIONARY, Alexander Schmidt. Full definitions, locations, shades of meaning in every word in plays and poems. More than 50,000 exact quotations. 1,485pp. 6½ x 9¼. 2-vol. set.
Vol. 1: 22726-X
Vol. 2: 22727-8

SELECTED POEMS, Emily Dickinson. Over 100 best-known, best-loved poems by one of America's foremost poets, reprinted from authoritative early editions. No comparable edition at this price. Index of first lines. 64pp. 5³⁄₁₆ x 8¼. 26466-1

THE INSIDIOUS DR. FU-MANCHU, Sax Rohmer. The first of the popular mystery series introduces a pair of English detectives to their archnemesis, the diabolical Dr. Fu-Manchu. Flavorful atmosphere, fast-paced action, and colorful characters enliven this classic of the genre. 208pp. 5³⁄₁₆ x 8¼. 29898-1

THE MALLEUS MALEFICARUM OF KRAMER AND SPRENGER, translated by Montague Summers. Full text of most important witchhunter's "bible," used by both Catholics and Protestants. 278pp. 6⅝ x 10. 22802-9

SPANISH STORIES/CUENTOS ESPAÑOLES: A Dual-Language Book, Angel Flores (ed.). Unique format offers 13 great stories in Spanish by Cervantes, Borges, others. Faithful English translations on facing pages. 352pp. 5⅜ x 8½. 25399-6

GARDEN CITY, LONG ISLAND, IN EARLY PHOTOGRAPHS, 1869–1919, Mildred H. Smith. Handsome treasury of 118 vintage pictures, accompanied by carefully researched captions, document the Garden City Hotel fire (1899), the Vanderbilt Cup Race (1908), the first airmail flight departing from the Nassau Boulevard Aerodrome (1911), and much more. 96pp. 8⅞ x 11¾. 40669-5

OLD QUEENS, N.Y., IN EARLY PHOTOGRAPHS, Vincent F. Seyfried and William Asadorian. Over 160 rare photographs of Maspeth, Jamaica, Jackson Heights, and other areas. Vintage views of DeWitt Clinton mansion, 1939 World's Fair and more. Captions. 192pp. 8⅞ x 11. 26358-4

CAPTURED BY THE INDIANS: 15 Firsthand Accounts, 1750-1870, Frederick Drimmer. Astounding true historical accounts of grisly torture, bloody conflicts, relentless pursuits, miraculous escapes and more, by people who lived to tell the tale. 384pp. 5⅜ x 8½. 24901-8

THE WORLD'S GREAT SPEECHES (Fourth Enlarged Edition), Lewis Copeland, Lawrence W. Lamm, and Stephen J. McKenna. Nearly 300 speeches provide public speakers with a wealth of updated quotes and inspiration–from Pericles' funeral oration and William Jennings Bryan's "Cross of Gold Speech" to Malcolm X's powerful words on the Black Revolution and Earl of Spenser's tribute to his sister, Diana, Princess of Wales. 944pp. 5⅜ x 8⅜. 40903-1

THE BOOK OF THE SWORD, Sir Richard F. Burton. Great Victorian scholar/adventurer's eloquent, erudite history of the "queen of weapons"–from prehistory to early Roman Empire. Evolution and development of early swords, variations (sabre, broadsword, cutlass, scimitar, etc.), much more. 336pp. 6⅛ x 9¼.
25434-8